GWENDOLYN GRACE

Katherine Hannigan

GREENWILLOW BOOKS
An Imprint of HarperCollins*Publishers*

*For Lauren, who asks and says, "Please,"
and for Meagan, who just does it*

Gwendolyn Grace
Copyright © 2015 by Katherine Hannigan.
All rights reserved. Manufactured in China.
For information address HarperCollins Children's Books,
a division of HarperCollins Publishers,
195 Broadway, New York, NY 10007.
www.harpercollinschildrens.com

Adobe Photoshop, 140-pound hot press Arches
watercolor paper, watercolor paints, and colored
pencils were used to create the full-color art.
The text type is Burbank Small PS.

Library of Congress Cataloging-in-Publication Data
Hannigan, Katherine.
Gwendolyn Grace / Katherine Hannigan.
pages cm
"Greenwillow Books."
Summary: Gwendolyn Grace, an alligator, does not
want to obey when her mother tells her to be quiet
while the baby is sleeping, but finally sees that being
patient has its rewards.
ISBN 978-0-06-234519-6 (hardcover)
[1. Babies–Fiction. 2. Noise–Fiction. 3. Patience–Fiction.
4. Sisters–Fiction. 5. Alligators–Fiction.] I. Title.
PZ7.H19816Gwe 2015 [E]–dc23 2014016527

15 16 17 18 19 SCP 10 9 8 7 6 5 4 3 2 1

First Edition

 Greenwillow Books

creak

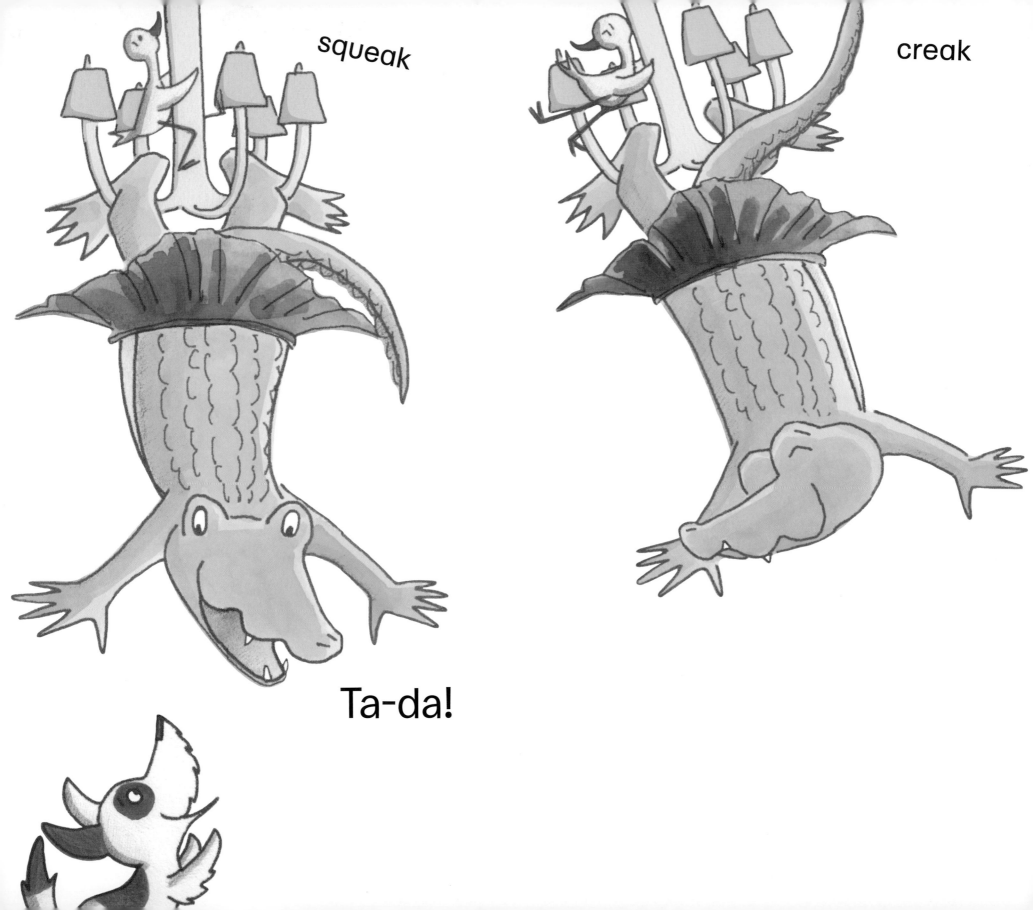

squeak

creak

Ta-da!

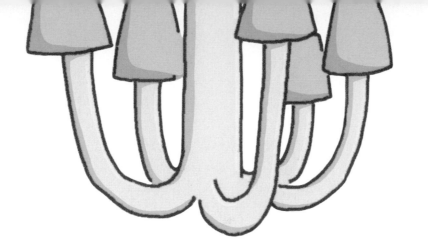

Yes?

Stop making so
much noise, *please*.
The baby is trying
to sleep.

Okay.

But . . .

do you mean . . .

stop making music in the kitchen?

CRASH!

ping
ping
ping

chicka-chicka-cha

All right.

Or . . .

do you mean . . .

Fine.

And . . .

do you mean . . .

quit playing chugga-choo-choo,

cut out the doggy dress-up,

and no more bouncing on the bed?

Sigh.
Gwendolyn Grace,
come here.

What now?

Gwendolyn Grace,
you have to be quiet
when the baby's sleeping.
Please whisper.

All right.

But Mama . . .

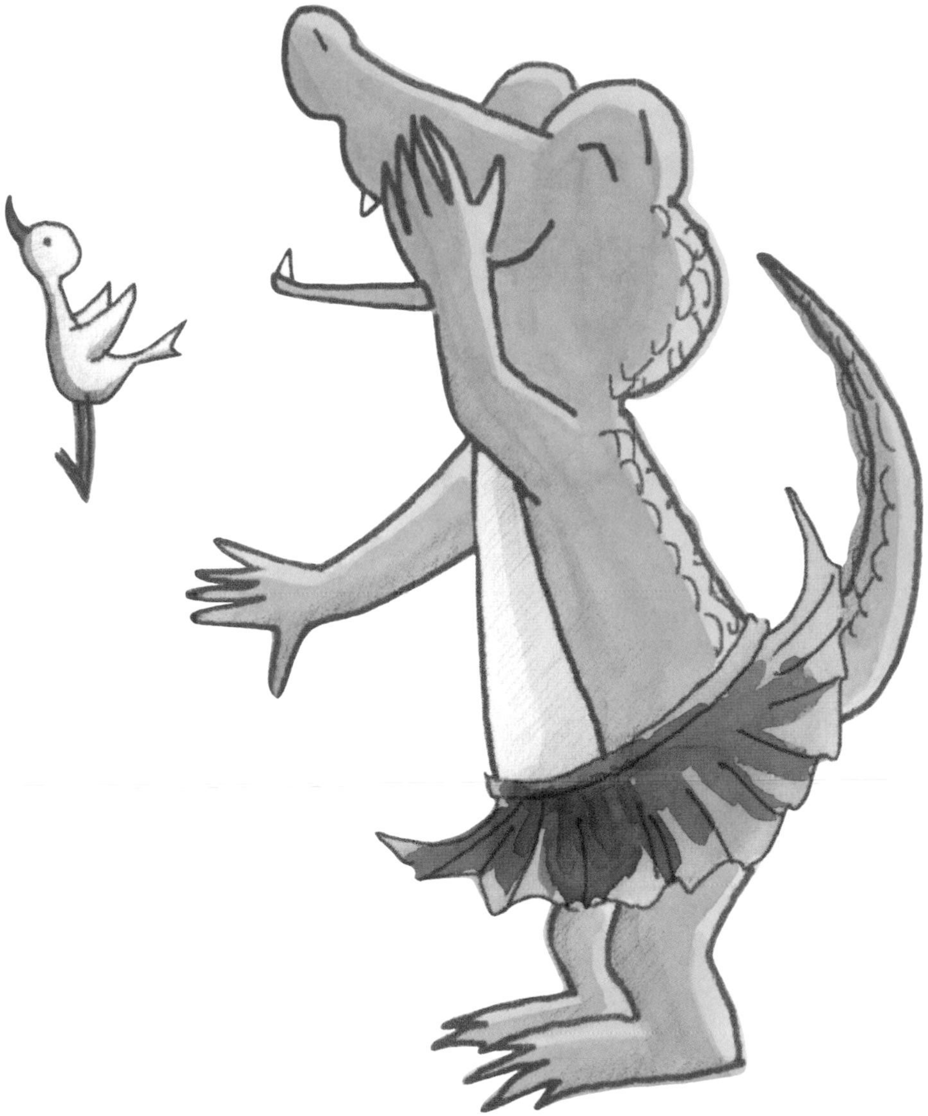

do you mean . . .

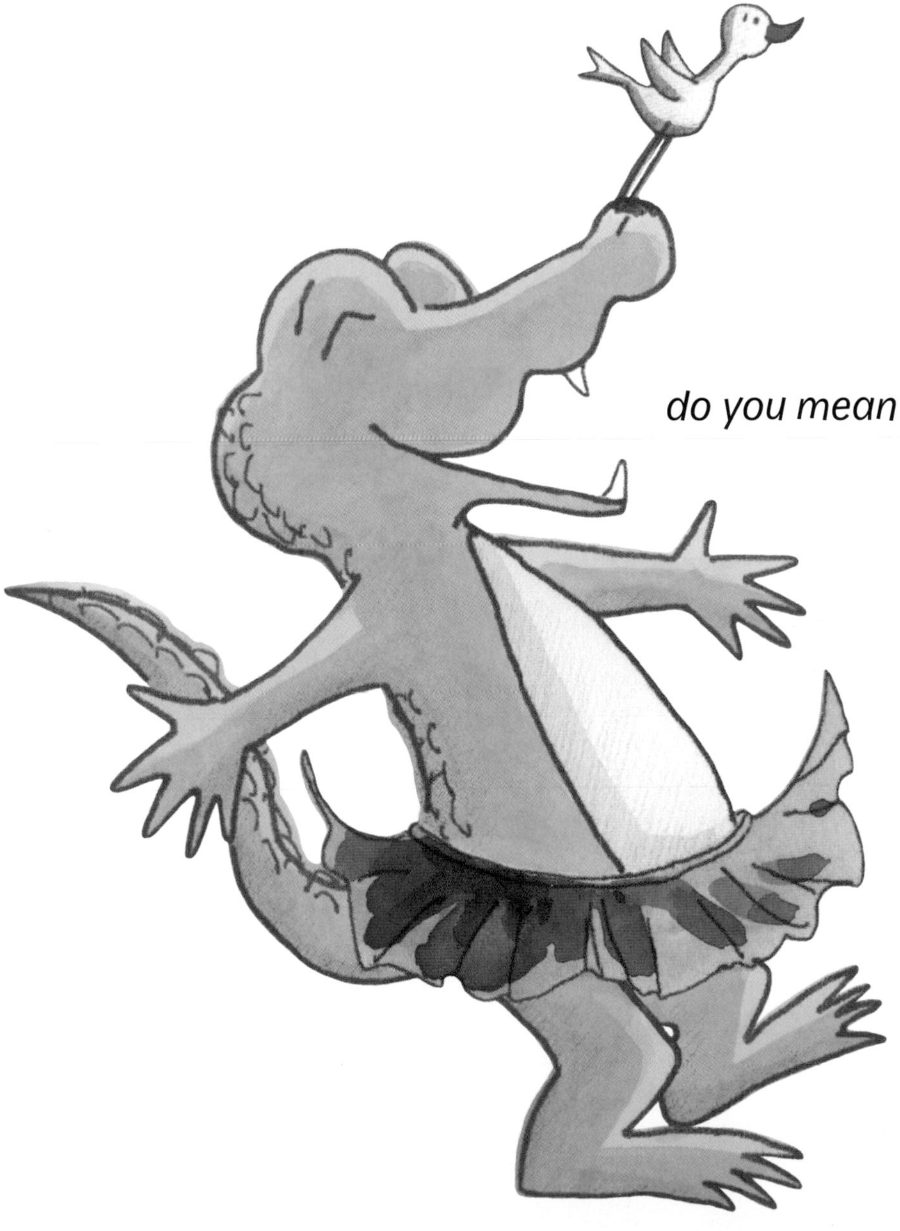

*when the baby
is done sleeping,
we can all play together?*

Yes.

Yay!